THE EMISSARY FROM MEZERITCH:
A DARK HASIDIC TALE

by

BARAK A. BASSMAN

TELEMACHUS PRESS

This book is a work of fiction. Names, characters, places and incidents are either the product of the author's imagination or are used fictitiously. Any resemblance to actual persons, living or dead, or to actual events or locales is entirely coincidental.

THE EMISSARY FROM MEZERITCH: A DARK HASIDIC TALE
Copyright © 2020 Barak A. Bassman. All rights reserved, including the right to reproduce this book, or portions thereof, in any form. No part of this text may be reproduced, transmitted, downloaded, decompiled, reverse engineered, or stored in or introduced into any information storage and retrieval system, in any form or by any means, whether electronic or mechanical without the express written permission of the author. The scanning, uploading, and distribution of this book via the Internet or via any other means without the permission of the author and publisher is illegal and punishable by law. Please purchase only authorized electronic editions and do not participate in or encourage electronic piracy of copyrighted materials.

The publisher does not have any control over and does not assume any responsibility for author or third-party websites or their content.

Cover designed by Telemachus Press, LLC

Cover art: Portrait of Baal Shem of London by John Singleton Copley (Public Domain)

Published by Telemachus Press, LLC
7652 Sawmill Road
Suite 304
Dublin, Ohio 43016
http://www.telemachuspress.com

ISBN: 978-1-951744-47-2 (eBook)
ISBN: 978-1-951744-48-9 (Paperback)

Library of Congress Control Number: 2020922698

Version 2020.11.16

Table of Contents

THE EMISSARY FROM MEZERITCH:
A DARK HASIDIC TALE

I. The Arrival

IT WAS A burning hot Friday afternoon in the *shtetl* of W. Reb Shimon, soaked in his own sweat, was lazily finishing his final chores before the onset of *Shabbat*: straightening up the tables and chairs in his small inn and tavern, counting and stowing away his coins, making sure there were enough oats in the stables to feed the horses of his guests.

But then he saw the most astonishing man walk across his threshold and sit down at one of his tables. This man was quite tall—he had to stoop awkwardly to walk through the doorway—but so slender that it seemed as if a light evening breeze would blow him away to Warsaw. He was also so pale that he could have been a corpse dug up from its grave, even though he must have been walking in the sun for hours because he was not accompanied by a coachman or a wagon driver. And finally, although his clothes were so threadbare that the stitches were visibly coming apart, he carried a leather bag of the most elaborate and ornate craftsmanship.

Reb Shimon stared at this stranger, unsure whether he was a real person or a fevered hallucination brought on by the terrible heat. The man stared back at him. Eventually the man picked up a small metal cup lying on the floor, threw it at Reb Shimon's head, and asked what a Jew needed to do to be served something to drink.

Reb Shimon quickly apologized and said that the heat had overcome him—who had ever been forced to endure such heat, as if the Holy One, Blessed be He, had decided to bake His poor Jews into little cakes for Him to eat.

Good sir, would you prefer ale or vodka? he asked the stranger.

Innkeeper, what is your name?

Reb Shimon, son of Reuven.

Then, my new friend Reb Shimon, pour me a glass of your finest Hungarian wine—a sweet Tokay to parch my thirst.

Shimon laughed to himself—this pale beggar, in his flimsy rags, wanted his most expensive wine—the barrels tapped only when the *Pan* or the *Pani* or some other wealthy lord or lady happened to visit his little inn. The wealthiest Jews in W. could not afford such luxury—yet this haughty *schlemiel* demanded to be served as if he were an Emperor.

Still, he thought, the stranger had been walking in the awful heat for some time and he was no doubt light-headed from exhaustion and thirst. So he tried to be reasonable and gentle with the man: Sir, such delicacies are not for when you are parched from the road—thirsty as you are now, you would gulp the wine down in a fast go, instead of savoring the fine flavors. *Nu*, let's share some ale before the *Shabbat* begins, and I will find you some bread and butter to fill your belly. Later tonight, after the evening prayers, you can sleep in a corner of my barn that catches the nighttime breeze.

The stranger bore his eyes into Reb Shimon. He had not looked closely at those huge black eyes before, but now they made his limbs quiver and his pulse race, so intense and angry was their glare.

The stranger then spoke again, in a firm, calm voice: Reb Shimon, kindly serve me a glass of Tokay. And also a few choice slices of brisket. Have your wife prepare for me your finest room, the one where your *Pan* and *Pani* stay when they deign to visit their subjects in this town.

Reb Shimon was unsure exactly what to say to this madman with the terrifying eyes, but then the stranger reached into his leather bag and pulled out a fistful of gold ducats, which he dropped on the table and pushed toward the innkeeper.

Shimon was astounded—he had never been paid so well for the middling accommodations and fare he could offer. Without another word, he scooped up the money and ran to his wife and daughter and told them to prepare the *Pan*'s room for a special wealthy guest. He then dashed to the cellar to pour the Tokay wine and to the kitchen to slice and plate the brisket.

Once he had served his guest, Reb Shimon sat down next to him and asked him his name and his business in W. The stranger, in between huge bites and long draughts—the man ate like he had been starving for months—replied: My name is Aharon, son of Y., from K. I travel among the holy communities of Poland to preach the words of the true Torah of the Holy One, Blessed be He. I am an emissary to all Jews from my master, the holy and learned Maggid of M., may his name be blessed and may his merit protect us.

What do you mean, the true Torah? Shimon asked him. Do you think the rest of us have spent our lives following some imposter Torah?

But Aharon did not reply.

Worried that his question may have been rude, and eager to ingratiate himself with his wealthy guest, Reb Shimon tried a different tack: Tell me, Reb Aharon the Emissary, why does a rich man like yourself travel with no coach, no driver, and no horses? Would it not be better to sit in a carriage, shielded from the sun, than to abuse your poor feet by walking so much? And aren't you scared of being robbed on the highway?

The love and presence of the Holy One, Blessed be He, is the only protection I need on the road. And to ride in a coach would be to separate myself from the glory and wonder of His Creation in favor of a stuffy, cramped wooden box fashioned by lowly men.

The sun was setting fast now, and Reb Shimon excused himself to change out of his dirty weekday clothes for the *Shabbat*. Once he was ready, he took his guest with him to the town's synagogue for the evening prayers. When Shimon greeted the other Jewish householders in the synagogue benches, he eagerly whispered into their ears about the mysterious visitor—how, although he dressed like a beggar and traveled on foot, he tossed about gold coins like the grandest magnate in Poland.

Though Shimon swayed and mumbled the Hebrew words of the prayers, his mind wandered far from holy things. He thought about the windfall he was making from Reb Aharon. If he could somehow convince Aharon to stay for a week, or a bit longer, he would make his entire annual lease payment for the inn. And there would be extra left over—he could add to his daughter's dowry, get her a better match when the time came to wed. Or even buy himself some new shoes.

But these happy fantasies of future wealth were interrupted by a sudden shouting and screaming—a joyous shouting, as if all of life's blessings had somehow just been granted to one man. Shimon turned his eyes toward the sound and saw, to his shock, that Reb Aharon had left his seat in the back of the synagogue and mounted the *bimah* in front, where he was dancing and singing and shouting in front of the Holy Ark that housed the community's Torah scrolls. Shimon tried to figure out what he was singing, but it was a hodgepodge of strange, guttural nonsense sounds. Still, there was certainly a melody, fast, rhythmic, that made his feet almost wish to jump up and dance, too.

Reb Aharon's behavior then grew even more bizarre. With his eyes closed tightly, he hugged and caressed and kissed the wooden ark and its velvet curtains. By this point, every other Jew in the synagogue had stopped his own prayers to gape at the madman's antics. Afraid someone might handle his guest roughly—and drive him, offended, away from the town of W., before he had spent more of his many ducats at the inn—Reb Shimon walked onto the *bimah*, took Aharon's hand, and led him gently down and back to his seat. The rest of the men resumed their prayers.

But then Shimon saw Reb Aharon leave his seat again—this time in the other direction, out the door. Shimon followed him outside. Aharon was skipping and dancing towards a broad meadow, where the flowers reflected the soft white moonlight. He jumped into the flower bed, like a mischievous little child, and writhed about, with a wide smile on his face and his black eyes fixed on the starry sky above. He burst out again singing the same fast-paced melody to a string of nonsense sounds.

Shimon was not sure what to do. He looked around—thankfully no one else had followed them. So perhaps it was best to let the madman have his fun. And Shimon remembered that glittering fistful of ducats: he was being well recompensed to look after this strange man.

After a lengthy period of time passed in this way, Reb Aharon stood up, brushed himself off, and spoke once more: Reb Shimon, let us return to the inn for the *Shabbat* evening meal.

After they had returned to the inn, Shimon's wife, Leah, pulled him aside to discuss their new guest. She had already heard gossip that this Reb Aharon had made a bizarre spectacle of himself in the synagogue. Was it safe to sleep under the same roof with him? Was he possessed by some demon or wandering spirit? And those ducats—wasn't her husband the least suspicious of how a beggar in rags had more wealth than the greatest lord? Did it not occur to him that maybe this treasure was stolen? That some angry

Pan, with his dogs and his guards and his pistols, might descend upon them in vengeance for the theft of his riches, and decide to loot and burn everything in the inn?

Reb Shimon knew her words were wise and sensible. But still, maybe they could hide the ducats and keep the madman at bay just until he left for the next *shtetl*. He said he was an emissary sent forth by his master to spread some teaching or other—he would no doubt be on his way soon enough in the hunt for more disciples.

So Shimon told his wife not to worry and that the stranger would be gone before she knew it. He urged her to remember that it was *Shabbat*, and that she should rest and be merry.

In the meantime, Reb Aharon had finished his meal. Shimon showed him to his room and helped him into bed.

II. The Shaming

EXHAUSTED FROM THE previous night's strange antics, Shimon woke later than usual and scrambled to dress and wash himself. But when he went to Reb Aharon's room, to give him some breakfast and escort him back to the synagogue for the morning prayers, Shimon found only an empty bed. The stranger must have run off in the night, he thought. Perhaps that was for the best—he had lucked into a few extra ducats, but who could feel safe sleeping under the same roof as that lunatic? Better he was gone to torment another innkeeper in another town.

Shimon joined his Leah for a quick breakfast. When she heard Aharon's bed was empty she sighed and smiled and gave thanks to *HaShem* for seeing them through the previous night's strange ordeal. Shimon said he looked forward to a long nap later that afternoon.

But when he entered the synagogue, there was Reb Aharon swaying under his prayer shawl and loudly chanting Psalms. Shimon pulled the beadle aside and asked when Aharon had arrived that morning.

Shortly after sunrise, the old beadle answered. He woke me from my slumbers, so eager was he to pray. The beadle went on to relate that Reb Aharon had also demanded permission to preach from the *bimah*, to share what he promised would be special and true words of Torah. When the town's rabbi later arrived to begin his prayers, the beadle had sought and received permission from him for the stranger to preach after the morning prayers had concluded.

How could you give him permission to preach? Shimon asked. Didn't you see him last night? I am sure he is a good man, but he seems … troubled, unwell.

But the beadle now looked at Shimon as if he were the most contemptible fool: Troubled? Unwell? So he was carried away with his love for the Holy One last night, is that some sort of sin? I am sure he will share fine and exalted words that will fill all of our hearts with love of Torah. And anyway, our rabbi deserves to rest, too, on this day of rest—the poor man is always being badgered for a lengthy discourse every *Shabbes* morning.

Worried about what Reb Aharon was going to say when the time came for him to preach to the congregation, Shimon had trouble concentrating on his prayers. His guest could not have had time to prepare a proper discourse by consulting the holy texts and learned commentaries in the town's *bet midrash*. Perhaps he had brought a discourse with him, some speech that he had copied out somewhere else on his travels? But Shimon had seen no such thing in Aharon's belongings—not even a stray, scribbled note of scholarship, much less a well-reasoned and closely argued interpretation of a difficult passage from the Talmud, of the kind that their rabbi would deliver for the town's edification.

The man was clearly unwell and needed to be shown kindness, compassion—and certainly not to be made a fool of in public by letting him babble on about who only knew what. A poor, suffering Jew, plainly afflicted by madness, was going to be shamed publicly because the rabbi was too lazy to offer a few words of Torah on this day.

But then again, Reb Shimon's thoughts continued, maybe Reb Aharon would deliver a simple homily, a touching tale of a holy sage of blessed memory that would be easy to understand and provide a pleasant moral. Was it so wrong to give him the chance to spread the little bit of wisdom and learning he had? And the rabbi did need to rest every now and then.

By the time that Reb Aharon mounted the *bimah* and leaned his long, skeletal arms over the lectern, Shimon was sure that the sermon to come would be short and harmless.

But Aharon did not launch into an uplifting tale from the saintly life of a holy sage of blessed memory. Instead, he silently stared at the congregation, his black eyes boiling with disgust. Under the weight of that intense glare, the gossiping, distracted men in the synagogue benches slowly quieted down until there was complete silence in the sanctuary.

Then the sermon finally began with a single word shouted out loud like a ball shot from a cannon: Liar!

And Reb Aharon pointed his bony finger at the town's rabbi.

That man is a liar, he continued. While he may spin his lies from the words of the holy sages, they are still lies. This false teacher urges you to fast and to weep and to rent your garments in atonement for your many sins. He lauds and exalts Jews who starve and torture themselves in order, supposedly, to cleanse themselves of sin and to become pure. He tells you that this world and its delights are snares and traps which must be escaped through mortification of the flesh, so the soul can ascend to the higher realms.

These are lies! Fasting and mortification are not the ways to seek the presence of the Holy One, Blessed be He. The Holy One is infinite and abounding, and His holy sparks of light are hidden everywhere in His glorious creation. You must join with Him, become one with Him, by embracing His presence all around you. Take joy—feel rapture—in everything around us and lose yourself in frenzied love of His glorious wine and sunshine and fresh, warm bread. When you fast, when you mortify and afflict yourself, you are tearing yourself away from the glory of the Creation of the Holy One, Blessed be He and severing your connection to Him.

He has given us the most beautiful carpet, the most intricately woven piece of craftsmanship—this carpet is the world He chose to create. We are each woven into this carpet, which is both His Creation and an extension of Himself. When you afflict yourself with fasting and mortification, you rip your patch of the carpet away from the rest and leave an unsightly tear and hole. Why is this? Because by believing you have done a righteous deed in rejecting the wonderful food and drink He has created for you, you exalt yourself as worthier than the rest of Creation and wallow in your own arrogant saintliness for having spurned what *HaShem* made for your enjoyment and bounty—and you thereby make your own so-called saintliness into the idol that you worship and bow down to.

At this point, the town's rabbi jumped to his feet and ordered Aharon to be silent. When the stranger ignored him and continued his preaching in the same vein, several burly men rose from the synagogue benches and forcibly dragged him down from the *bimah*.

Shimon followed the crowd as Aharon was pulled outside the synagogue and pinned to the ground in the outer courtyard. He saw the rabbi spit several times in Aharon's face, followed by many other Jewish householders who did the same.

One or two men kicked him.

And then came the final, and worst, humiliation: a stray black dog approached Aharon and urinated on his waist and thighs.

The Jewish householders laughed cruelly and pointed as they watched the dog finish his business. The rabbi then ordered him to leave town and never to return.

Reb Aharon rose slowly, with deliberate, stiff movements, and wiped himself off. Without speaking another word, he returned to the inn (with Shimon in tow), retrieved his belongings, and left on foot, following the main road out of town.

III. Retribution

THE NEXT FEW days passed easily for Reb Shimon: traveling merchants lodged at the inn, peasants guzzled his alcohol, and his Leah kvetched about this or that in the kitchen or the stables. The memory of Reb Aharon and his bizarre behavior began to fade, although a couple of drunk peasants toasted the mad Jewish beggar who had danced in the fields and then insulted the rabbi.

But matters took an unexpected turn for the worse later in the week as the next *Shabbat* approached. The problems started with the milk. Leah had gone out to buy milk from their neighbors who kept goats, but she returned to Shimon empty-handed, explaining to him that those goats no longer had any milk in them. Shimon suggested several other households where goats or cows were kept, both Jewish and Gentile, but wherever she went there was no milk—all the udders in the *shtetl* had completely dried up at the exact same time.

That night, in the synagogue, Reb Shimon heard the same complaint from the other Jewish householders: there was no milk to be had. And nobody could explain what had happened. The men who kept goats or cows said that one day they gave milk, but the next morning they were withered and dried—as if milk had been removed from the world by some strange decree.

So Shimon and Leah, like the other householders, passed the *Shabbat* eating only meat and vegetable dishes, figuring that they would switch to dairy later in the week when the milk flowed again.

But as the days rolled on, there was still no milk.

And then the town's animals—not just the goats and the cows this time, but also the chicken and the geese, and even the dirty stray cats and the brown field mice—began to walk sluggishly, lose their appetite, and fall down on the ground moaning in pain.

The animals' skins burst with sores, greenish, bulbous, and oozing thick white pus with a nauseating smell. The town's Jews barricaded themselves in their homes and shut their windows to escape the stench, but the smell still snaked in through the slightest cracks in the walls, and the houses echoed loudly with the sounds of vomiting.

But then the horrible smell vanished as suddenly as it had arrived.

Reb Shimon wondered if some enterprising Jew had disposed of the rotting animals, perhaps burning them in a heap somewhere outside the town. He thought about the cost of replacing all those dead chickens, geese, goats, and cows. Jewish householders would need loans to buy so much new livestock all at once, and he still had that pile of gold ducats from the mad Reb Aharon—maybe this was an opportunity, yes a real opportunity. Money begets money, he reminded himself.

Shimon stepped around his still snoring Leah and walked out onto the veranda to see what had happened.

There were no people about. The animals were still lying in the road, but they were now clearly dead. Huge birds, with pitch black feathers, were swooping down from the white clouds and gobbling up large chunks of the corpses.

One of these birds landed near Shimon's inn to feast upon a dead goat covered in sores. It turned its head sideways and glared into Shimon's eyes. His blood went cold and his limbs froze as he looked back into the bird's eyes; he thought they were filled with anger and accusation, as if he had committed some horrible, unspeakable sin.

Once the birds had eaten their fill, there were only a few scattered bones left about, which the town's Jews easily collected and burned. As Shimon had correctly guessed, there was now a dire need for loans to purchase new livestock, and he shrewdly exploited the opportunity to become a new partner in several poultry and dairy businesses.

The next *Shabbat* was peaceful. There were geese and chicken again for Friday night dinner, and milk for dairy dishes the day after. At the synagogue, there were many prayers of sincere gratitude to the Holy One, Blessed be He, for the community's deliverance from the bizarre plague that had afflicted the beasts and birds.

But this happiness was not to last. A couple of days into the next week, Leah pulled Shimon aside to tell him that their daughter Miriam had fallen ill—fever, retching, chills, and a hacking cough that sounded as if she were trying to expel an army of demons from inside her chest.

Shimon went into town to buy medicine and look for a doctor. But the apothecary threw his hands in the air in response to Shimon's request for help. What am I to do? he asked. Every Jew in this town has come to my shop this morning, seeking medicine, seeking doctors, and every Jew says his child burns with fever and coughs wretchedly. All the children are afflicted, and there is only so much medicine that I can keep in stock at one time—these medicines cost money to buy, so much money, and I am no emperor with sacks of gold and silver to toss about as I please. So, Reb Shimon, I wish I could help, but I have no more medicine to sell you. Go home, give your poor girl some broth, and come back tomorrow or the next day—maybe I will have more medicine by then. How was I supposed to know that every child would get sick on the same day? Who could have imagined such a thing?

On his way back to the inn, Shimon stopped at the house of one of his new partners in the poultry business, to get fresh chicken feet for some broth for his Miriam. But when Shimon entered, his partner immediately fell upon Shimon's shoulder and wept uncontrollably. His three sons had fallen terribly ill, he said, and the youngest, who was only four years old, had already passed into the next world. The man's wife was sewing a child-sized funeral shroud, and the burial society had dropped off a miniature coffin for the tiny corpse.

As Shimon soon learned, this was not the only child who had died. For the next few days there was a steady procession of sad, quiet men and wailing, gesticulating women carrying little wooden caskets to the cemetery to bury their offspring who had departed from this life.

When the doctors eventually arrived in town to examine the sick children, they were baffled—they swore they had never seen such a disease. They tried one remedy after another—phials of strangely colored potions, herbs pressed against body parts, bloodletting, leeches—but nothing made the slightest difference. The distraught parents drove the doctors away and cursed them as quacks and thieves who had stolen their money and done more harm than good.

The town's rabbi ordered a three-day fast. All the men were to pray and study in the synagogue, begging the Holy One, Blessed be He, for forgiveness, mercy, and the health of their children. The women were ordered to recite prayers of their own in Yiddish, to be led by the rabbi's wife. The town's Jews rent their garments and wailed their hearts out and starved their bellies, making their own dwindling flesh into a sacrificial offering to atone for the great and many sins that had, no doubt, caused such a terrible calamity to befall their sons and daughters.

But it was all to no avail.

In answer to spreading rumors of the awful sickness that had afflicted the town's children, wonder working itinerant kabbalists, *baalei shem*, descended upon the town and packed the rooms in Shimon's inn. These men were pale and gaunt from years of fasting—they rarely, if ever, ate between one *Shabbat* and the next, and even then just a few bites of bread or sips of broth. They were famous for their extraordinary piety, studying esoteric, mystical texts day and night, and forcing themselves to undergo extreme acts of mortification—rolling naked in the snow, submerging their hands in boiling water—in order to beg forgiveness for the sins that had so bitterly lengthened the years of Israel's exile and prevented the *Mashiach* from riding forth to bring redemption to the world.

These skeletal saints, with trembling hands and watery, saucer-like eyes, now devoted their prayers and rites to the well-being of the town's children. They furiously scribbled amulets containing powerful and mysterious combinations of the hidden true names of the Holy One, Blessed be He, and His mightiest angels. With quivering limbs, they paced around the children's beds reciting incantations and loudly blowing the *shofar* to cast out the demons that had brought the terrible sickness upon the town.

Yet … still … nothing worked.

One night, shortly after midnight, Shimon was violently woken by his wife, Leah. She was a disheveled wreck—her wig was askew, her kerchief ripped, and her face covered in tracks of dried tears. She was moaning and scratching herself so violently that blood leaked out from her skin in several places.

He asked her: Leah, what has happened?

Please forgive me, she began. I know it was a terrible sin, but what was I to do? I don't want our Miriam to die, but she is so pale, and her chest rattles so horribly when she coughs. I have fasted and prayed, I have put amulets around her neck and mine, but, because of my many sins, my prayers cannot reach the Throne of Glory in the highest heavens.

I did not know what else to do.

Earlier today, as the sun was setting, Beyle came to see me. Her husband does business with the convent near the *Pan*'s manor house. I forget what he sells them, but anyway, he does business with the Sisters and knows what they do to heal the sick. When doctors and prayers and fasts do not work, the Abbess will turn a sick child over to one particular elderly nun whose cell is located far away from the other Sisters. This elderly nun then takes the child into the woods at midnight. These children are then always healed the next day, but the Abbess does not permit any questions about how it was done.

Beyle's Yankel has been sick like our Miriam, so she visited the convent and asked to speak to the elderly nun. At first, she would not divulge her secret, but when Beyle swore to become a Christian if her son's life were saved, the old nun relented and told her how she travels to a hut in the woods where an old witch lives. This witch knows many ancient, secret truths which have been forgotten by others—old ways from the *goyim* in these lands, from before they were Christians. She told Beyle how to go there.

Beyle was scared to go by herself, and she begged me to accompany her. How could I refuse the plea of a mother fighting for her son's life? And I figured maybe I could help our Miriam, too. Maybe this was the miracle I had prayed for. After all, King Saul—may his merit protect us—sought guidance from the witch of Endor.

Once everyone was asleep we crept into the forest, following the path that Beyle had been told to follow, until we reached a hut in a clearing. There was a dim light from inside, and the smell of roasting meat.

Beyle knocked on the door. A short, fat peasant woman with three hairy moles on her face answered and invited us inside. Beyle told her about our children and what the old nun had said to her. The woman asked if we could pay, and we said yes.

Then the woman moved her spit of meat away from the fire, and put a big round pot in its place. Into this pot she poured all sorts of strange things—green and blue liquids, dead bats, dead frogs, gigantic spiders and hissing snakes, which she boiled alive in front of our eyes—and she sang, too, in this horrible, squeaking voice, songs in a language I had never heard before.

After a while, she told us everything was ready. She explained that she would look into the pot, which would reveal to her, in its special way, the exact malady afflicting our children and the proper blend of herbs to heal them. I was so full of hope—I was sure I was about to get the cure for my Miriam.

So the witch leaned over her pot, muttering more incomprehensible words in her language. Then she grew quiet. Beyle gripped my hand tightly—everything was so quiet—you have never heard such quiet in your life.

And then the witch screamed. She sounded like someone had just thrown boiling water into her eyes. She jumped up, still screaming, and ran in a crazy circle around the hut, covering her eyes, knocking over her pots and phials and whatnot.

When she had finally calmed down, she pleaded with us to leave and never come back. She broke down in tears and asked why we had brought such evil to her, she was a good woman, a kind woman, she healed children. She kept asking: Why would we do this to her?

So Beyle asked her: But what did we do? We only want to help our children.

But the old witch would not answer. She just screamed some more and cast us out of her hut.

I am so sorry. Shimon, please pray, fast, beg the Holy One, Blessed be He, not to punish our child for the terrible sin of idolatry I committed tonight. I could not bear it if my sin killed my beautiful Miriam.

Shimon held his crying wife in his arms and rocked her gently. His limbs felt heavy and, no matter how hard he tried, his thoughts refused to form clearly in his weary mind.

IV. The Burning of the Idols

REB SHIMON, LIKE all the town's Jewish householders, had abandoned the things of this world to devote his time to prayer in the synagogue, begging the Holy One, Blessed be He, to lift the curse upon their children. Everything had become blurry and dizzy to him, as he—like the others—went days without eating, convinced by their rabbi that only the most extreme penitential fasting could lift the cruel decree that had issued forth from the Heavenly Court. But their pious devotions brought no relief from suffering—to the contrary, their sufferings were about to increase yet again.

This next calamity fell upon their heads in the middle of the week, at twilight. Shimon had collapsed, exhausted, upon a bench in the synagogue; he had dropped his *tefillin* onto the floor but lacked the energy to find them and pick them up. All he could think about was how desperately he longed for Friday night when, at last, the rabbi would permit him to break the week's fast and eat again. His head slid down his chest and his eyelids felt heavy as he fantasized about the taste of fresh, soft bread in his mouth.

But then a scream woke him up. In the back of the synagogue, someone was shouting about a fire. Shimon roused himself and followed the crowd outside. He saw three pillars of smoke rising to the sky, one nearby, and two farther off in the direction of the *Pan*'s estates in the countryside.

Stumbling forward, Shimon went to the town square where he saw an astounding sight: the church was burning to the ground, but the fire was not spreading to any of the other buildings. The priest was frantically running in and out of the building to save his books and statues and relics, and the town's Christians poured bucket after bucket of water onto the inferno, but the fire kept raging, undiminished, until the church had been reduced to a compact lump of ashes and rubble.

Yet the fire never spread, not even to the wooden buildings which were right next to the church. And once the destruction of the church was complete, the fires mysteriously vanished.

Weeping over the rubble, the priest turned his ire toward Shimon and the other Jews standing near him: This was no ordinary fire, he said. Somehow this fire could only burn our holy church. You dirty, disgusting *żyds* have always hated our beautiful Lord Jesus Christ. You humiliated and murdered Him when He walked the Earth, and now you have used black magic—your filthy *Kabbalah*—to destroy His church here. But the *Pan* is no Pilate: he will not wash his hands of your crimes and look the other way. He is a good Christian and he will defend the honor of his Lord and Savior.

Shimon walked quickly back to the inn. He told his Leah what had happened and that he feared for their lives. They should flee, now, that very night, while they still could.

But how can we flee? Leah said. Look at our Miriam, her soul barely clings to her body, she is so sick and weak. A journey would kill her. And anyway, fires happen, *nu*, isn't that so? Is this the first time that a fire burned a building down? There is nothing magical about a fire. So the town got lucky that the fire did not spread—is that a cause for alarm? We should celebrate and thank *HaShem* for keeping the fire from consuming everything in sight—perhaps your prayers are finally being heard, perhaps the fire not spreading will be the beginning of the lifting of whatever harsh decree is tormenting us. You will see, Shimon, it will be fine. Better than fine. The *goyim* will calm down and just rebuild their church.

Seeing Leah could not be persuaded to take the danger seriously, Shimon chose not to argue with her any further and went to bed.

The next morning there was a knock at the door. A rough broad-shouldered drunk named Ivan told Shimon that the *Pan* demanded his presence at the manor house immediately. Still rubbing the sleep from his eyes, and with his head pounding from the angry barking of Ivan's dog, Shimon found himself shoved into the back of a wagon with several other drowsy Jewish householders. Ivan then rounded up the rabbi and drove the group of Jews to the countryside.

When they arrived at the *Pan*'s manor house, Ivan kicked and shoved Shimon and the other Jewish householders inside and towards the drawing room. There they found the *Pan*, his pale blue eyes trembling with rage. His wife, the *Pani*, a sour, stout woman, stood to one side of him. The town priest stood on his other side. There were also nuns milling about the room, but Shimon did not recognize any of them.

The *Pan* explained that there had been three fires the previous night: not only the fire in town that had burned down the church, but also a fire that had burned down the private family chapel of the *Pan* and *Pani* and a third fire that had burned down the convent, which the noble family had endowed and supported on their lands for many generations. All three fires, the *Pan* continued, were suspiciously similar: they raged ferociously, impervious to the water being heaped upon them, until they had burned down a Christian holy place, and then they suddenly vanished. And none of the fires had spread to any other buildings or fields.

He, and his wife, and the priest, and the Abbess of the convent, and every other good Christian to whom he had spoken, were in agreement that these were no ordinary fires, but dark magic emanating from Satanic powers. And who besides the Jews, the wicked, shameless, and unrepentant killers of Christ Himself, would have wished to desecrate God's works so wantonly? The nature of the crime made their collective guilt all too obvious, and the *Pan* would not waste his time interrogating his filthy *żyds* to discover which one of them had uttered which particular malicious incantation. Suffice to say, there was no point in them trying to deny their crimes. The only appropriate question was the fitting punishment.

At first, the *Pan* had wanted to hang all the town's Jews. But the *Pani*, he said, whose tender heart has the boundless compassion of the Holy Virgin Mother, begged him not to and reminded him that each filthy *żyd* had been endowed with an immortal soul and free will, and thus there was still a chance they could repent and accept baptism. Heeding her earnest pleas, he had decided to spare their lives.

Shimon stole a glance at the *Pani*, hoping to catch a reassuring glimpse of this great compassion in her eyes. But she stared out stone-faced beneath the heavy folds of fat on her face.

The *Pan* continued: Because death was out of the question, he had decided upon a fine. The greedy *żyds* love money more than life itself, he reasoned, so a hefty fine would be a fate worse than death to them. Thus, he hereby ordered the town's Jews to pay all of the money necessary to rebuild the Christian holy places they had conjured to burn down, plus an additional amount equal to three times those costs in order to fund the endowment of new churches and monasteries.

Shimon felt as if Ivan had slammed a huge fist into his belly: there was simply not enough wealth in the Jewish community to pay this fine, even if they gave away all that they had, coins, houses, barrels of wine, everything, it would not be enough. They were ruined—they would be beggars, and his Miriam, even if she survived her illness, would never have a dowry and would die an old maid. He would have no grandson to say *Kaddish* for his soul someday.

The town's rabbi now stepped forward, in a posture of humble supplication. Great and mighty *Pan*, he began, we are but your meek and grateful servants. We understand your terrible, tragic loss, and we will pray …

But at this point the *Pan* turned his head to Ivan in the back of the room and whistled loudly. Ivan then let go of his dog's leash and the vicious animal lunged at the old rabbi, biting his buttocks and drawing blood. The rabbi cried out in the pain and tried to flee, but the dog chased him in a circle around the room. The *Pan* and Ivan hooted and laughed and encouraged the dog to bite off different pieces of the rabbi's body. The rabbi begged the *Pan* to stop, but this only made him laugh harder.

Eventually the *Pani* shouted that this silly and disgraceful spectacle must stop at once. Ivan then called the dog back to him, tied his leash back on, and went outside.

The *Pan* smirked at the rabbi. Once again, *zyd*, he said, the *Pani*'s kind heart has saved you. Now go, and speak no more of your sniveling lies to me. You have a month to pay what is due. Fail to pay and you must leave my lands and forfeit your property.

V. A Message from the Heavenly Court

LATER THAT DAY, Shimon fought bitterly with his Leah. He told her what the *Pan* had said and decreed, and what grave threats now hung over the heads of the town's Jews, and insisted again that flight was the only option. It is only a matter of time before they become violent, he said, so we should gather our money before it is seized and flee far away from here while we still can. Shimon reminded her of his wealthy cousin in Lithuania, who perhaps could help them.

But Leah would not hear of it. Miriam was too sick for a journey, she said. Nothing will happen for a month, which will give her time to heal and gather her strength. And maybe the evil decree will be lifted. The *Pan* has changed his mind before. And if he is drunk enough, he does not care about his Church.

This argument repeated itself, again and again, until Shimon, utterly worn down, found a dry pile of hay in his barn to sleep on—his own bed being too close to Leah, whose stubbornness he cursed with his fading breaths.

The next morning Shimon was again awakened early by a visitor, but this time it was the *shammes* (sexton) of the synagogue.

Reb Shimon, he said, wash and dress yourself. The rabbi wishes to see you immediately.

Before I can even say my morning prayers? Shimon asked.

There is no time to waste, the *shammes* insisted. The matter is urgent.

Can you at least tell me what this is about, so I can put my thoughts in order? Half of my soul is still trying to wiggle back into my body after wandering away last night.

Hurry up, the *shammes* replied. There are others to be summoned as well. You know what you need to know—that you need to wash, dress, and go immediately to the rabbi's house.

In short order Shimon found himself in the rabbi's cramped, dusty study, piled high with decaying books and strewn about scraps of Hebrew correspondence. The old rabbi looked quite small beneath these mountains of yellowing papers. The thick curtains were drawn tightly, and the only light was a dim candle on the rabbi's desk.

With Shimon were the same Jewish householders whom the *Pan* had summoned the day before.

Dear friends, the rabbi began, thank you for coming to visit me so early this morning. We have all been greatly troubled by the sufferings that have been visited upon us for our many sins—first the misery of our children, and now this new harsh decree from the *Pan* that you heard yesterday from his own lips, may that wretched Haman be cursed to wither and rot.

For many days, I have worried that our prayers have lacked the strength to reach as high as the Throne of Glory. Maybe some greedy, faithless man was secretly breaking his fast, or thinking sinful thoughts about his Gentile maidservant instead of concentrating upon the words of atonement that passed through his lips.

And perhaps that was true, at first. But as the days wore on, and our wretchedness grew, I could hear how genuine was your remorse for your sins and your pitiful pleas for forgiveness. I could see plainly how your bodies had weakened and wasted away from fasting. But still, the Heavenly Court would not lift the terrible decrees against us.

How, I asked myself, could the Holy One, Blessed be He, be so cruel to His children Israel? How could a father feel no compassion in his heart when he sees his children wasting away and hears their pleas for mercy? While we are not saints, we are hardly great sinners. We sin the way everyone sins—a little here and a little there, a prayer rushed through, a mistake made about whether a chicken we ate was truly kosher. But why should we merit such extraordinary punishment? After all, the Holy One promised Abraham that he would spare Sodom and Gomorrah for the sake of ten righteous men. Don't we have ten righteous souls in our town?

After we had escaped the house of the *Pan*—may his life be short and wretched, and end speedily and in our days—I spent the rest of my time yesterday in this room searching the words of the holy sages and the learned commentators for the wisdom to understand what is happening to us. Yet the harder I looked, and the more I exerted myself, the less I understood. Finally, in my frustration, I broke down and wept. And then exhausted from my weeping, I fell asleep.

But before my eyes closed, I had just enough strength remaining to utter a prayer begging that the soul of my righteous grandfather, a great scholar of the Torah and a pillar of his generation, should come to me in my dream and reveal the truth of what has been happening to us.

As sleep overcame me, everything was dark before my eyes, but then there was a light and I found myself in the synagogue in the *shtetl* where I had lived as a boy, before I left to study in the *yeshiva* of Z. I heard the sounds of prayer above me and looked up to see my grandfather swaying back and forth, wrapped in his *tallis* and *tefillin*. I realized I had become a small boy again. I reached up with my tiny fingers and tugged the strings of his *tallis* to get his attention.

He stopped praying and sat down next to me.

Zayde, I asked him, why has the wrath of the Holy One, Blessed be He, fallen so harshly upon me? What great sin have I committed, and what penance must I make?

Yankele, he said to me, I have seen your suffering and I have ascended to the Heavenly Court to intercede on your behalf. I seized the hems of the garments of the accusing angels and cursed them with terrible combinations of secret divine names to compel them to reveal what was your crime and what must be the atonement.

The accusing angels trembled and pleaded for mercy. They told me your sin—and your sin indeed was grave. But they also said that until you sought out my soul to guide you back to the path of righteousness, the truth of the matter would continue to be concealed from your wicked eyes.

But now that you have returned to your *zayde*, my Yankele— and here he pinched my cheeks and rubbed my hair—I will reveal to you what must be done.

You have wronged and humiliated a wondrous saint, a re- markable holy *tzaddik*, whose merit is so extraordinary that the angels wait impatiently each day for his glorious soul to return to them in the World to Come. Your penance is to find this *tzaddik* and show him the honor that is his due. You must fall at his feet and beg his forgiveness—you must admit to him that you under- stand how shameful was your conduct.

But *zayde*, I asked, who is this *tzaddik*?

Think, Yankele, search your memory. Have you shamed any scholar?

And then I remembered our strange visitor, who had jumped about and squawked like a madman and who had mounted the lectern to heap insults upon my head. Could this be the man? But he had shamed me, shamed all of us, with his words and his actions. And how could such a wild man be a *tzaddik*, a pillar of his generation?

So I asked my *zayde*: You cannot mean the madman who danced around the synagogue like a deranged chicken and then shamed me with his contemptuous words? He is the only man whom I have dishonored, but his punishment was fitting for the disrespect he showed to me. He should burn in *gehenna*, not receive a golden seat in the Celestial Academy in Paradise.

Once I had finished speaking, my grandfather struck me hard across the face. Even though it was only a dream, the pain still felt like the fiery lashes of a thousand accusing angels.

You idiot, he thundered at me, that man was the holy *tzaddik* about whom the angels sing their praises. He was teaching you, not insulting you, but you were too foolish and arrogant to grasp the depth and profundity of his Torah.

And now you dare to compare him to a chicken? He danced for joy because he had been seized with such overflowing love for the Holy One, Blessed be He, that he was no longer bound to the lowly material world. His love was like the love that King David felt when he danced before the Ark of the Covenant and sang his Psalms with joy bursting from his heart.

But you are no King David, no, your soul root seems to be the same as Michal, the haughty princess of King Saul, who despised and mocked King David. And in punishment for her contempt of David's love for *HaShem*, the Heavenly Court decreed that her womb would be closed, and she would be barren for all her days.

And so it is with you and the wicked householders of your *shtetl*: for the grave sin of shaming a holy *tzaddik*, you, like Michal, will lose the blessing of children. There will be no one left to say *Kaddish* for your putrid, filthy souls when you die and receive your just reckonings.

That is your fate—unless you cease with your silly and vain fasting and Psalm singing, and genuinely and truly repent your actual sins.

No more am I permitted to say.

Then my *zayde* disappeared, the light in my dream went out, and I awoke.

Thanks to my grandfather of blessed memory, whose merit protects us, we now know what must be done. We must atone for shaming this holy *tzaddik*. We must find him, beg him to return to our town, and seek his forgiveness.

Reb Shimon, you hosted him at your inn and you alone did not shame him. You should therefore be our intermediary. Go at once and find the *tzaddik*. I will give you money, several days' food, and use of a horse and wagon. I will send my wife to explain matters to your Leah, so do not worry on that account either.

Now go.

And so Reb Shimon found himself placed on a wagon with a surly Gentile driver, even though the fog of sleep had still not yet entirely lifted from his head. As the horse pulled them away, he offered a quiet prayer for guidance and good fortune on his journey.

VI. The Tzaddik's Second Sight

SHIMON TRAVELED ALL that day on the main road leading out of the *shtetl*, heading in what he thought he recalled was the direction that Reb Aharon had taken. His heart was heavy: He was frightened that, if he should fail to find the offended *tzaddik*, the town's children—including his Miriam—would never get well. And there would also be no hope of averting the *Pan*'s cruel decree and crippling fine.

He stopped every Jew and peasant whom he encountered, and asked them if they had met a Reb Aharon or had seen a man who fit his description. But the answer was always the same: no one knew or had met such a man. By nightfall, Shimon despaired of ever finding the *tzaddik* in time to save the town's Jews.

As the twilight was fading into night, he saw there was an inn not too far off on the side of the road. He told the driver to take the wagon there. When they arrived, Shimon approached the inn-keeper, a kindly old Jew.

Shalom aleichem, he greeted the old man.

Aleichem shalom, the man responded. How can I be of service to such a fine guest, eh?

A warm bed, a plate of bread and onions, and a drop of mead, if you please.

Of course, of course, come this way.

The innkeeper led Shimon inside his tavern and yelled at a young woman—his daughter perhaps?—to bring bread, onions, mead, and a little *kugel* too for the gentleman.

Shimon sat down at a small wooden table. The room seemed to him to be filled mostly with belching and burping peasants arguing loudly with each other. He saw that his driver had apparently found several friends, or at least congenial enough fellows with whom he could scratch his armpits and drink himself into a stupor.

Once the food was served, the innkeeper sat down next to Shimon. *L'Chaim*! he shouted although Shimon was too tired and sad to raise his cup to the toast.

Why are you so glum? he asked Shimon. My Raizl cooks the best *kugel* in all of Poland—you are lucky to have arrived when she has just made a fresh batch, and luckier still that my appetite isn't what it once was—when I was young like you, so long ago, I would have devoured the whole thing myself.

Thank you, friend, the *kugel* is excellent. But I am troubled. I am looking for this man, you see, who left my *shtetl* a short while ago heading in this direction. It is of the utmost importance that I find him—a matter of life and death for many, many Jews. But I have had no luck so far.

Tell me, young man, what does this fellow look like? Perhaps he passed through here.

So Shimon described Reb Aharon in as much detail as he could recall.

The old innkeeper smacked the table and broke into such wild laughter that he nearly fell out of his chair. Once he had pulled himself together again, he asked Shimon to excuse him for a minute.

The innkeeper then disappeared through a backdoor into the kitchen. He returned almost instantly, leading none other than Reb Aharon himself to Shimon's table.

Would you believe it, the innkeeper said, this Reb Aharon arrived here last night and told me that a sad, despairing man fitting your exact description would come looking for him. He was in the kitchen sampling the honey cakes as they came out of the oven—more of Raizl's delicacies, she could have cooked for King Solomon and the Queen of Sheba—and he had told me to come get him after you had arrived, but not until you had specifically asked if I had seen a man fitting his description. This is clearly a blessing from the Holy One, Blessed be He, bringing you two fine Jews together. Since your meeting has been arranged in the higher realms, I will leave you two alone to do whatever it is you are supposed to do with each other.

The innkeeper walked away, still chuckling to himself and slapping his thigh playfully.

Reb Aharon now sat down, grabbed Shimon's mug, mumbled a blessing, and drank all the mead. When he was finished, he put the empty mug back down again on the table, wiped his lips with his sleeve, and belched loudly.

Shimon was dumbfounded. He had not expected that Reb Aharon would have gone looking for *him*—and, to boot, would somehow know just where and when to find him. Having achieved his goal so suddenly and unexpectedly, he was not sure what to say or do.

While Shimon groped for the right words of greeting, Reb Aharon leaned back in his seat, let his arm dangle to the ground, and spoke first: Reb Shimon, it is truly a pleasure to see you again. When I stayed in W., you alone showed me the honor that I was due, even though you understood nothing of my Torah. I know why you are here. I know all about the illnesses that have plagued your children. And I also know about the wicked *Pan* and his cruel persecutions. Indeed, after seeing your town's many punishments for having shamed me, I pitied you and so I humbly beseeched the soul of your rabbi's grandfather to aid his blind grandson, who could not see the penance that was required of him and his flock. Left to his own devices, that imbecile would have let every child in W. waste away and die while he congratulated himself for his heroic piety in endlessly fasting and moaning Psalms.

Shimon felt uneasy—this was not the conversation he had anticipated. He tried to speak: But how ... but how could you know ...

But how could I know? Reb Aharon repeated. Surely you can't expect me to reveal every hidden mystery to you right here and now? Let me put it this way: When the Holy One, Blessed be He, contracted His infinite presence to make space in the universe for this world to be created, there was then a special light, different than any light you have ever seen from the sun or the moon or from burning candles. That first primordial light was so wondrous that with it you could see clear from one end of the universe to the other. And the light carried not only sights for the eyes to see, but words to hear and scents to smell. This is still the light that they use in the Heavenly Court to watch events unfold in the lower worlds.

From years of study with my master and teacher, the holy Maggid of M., the greatest *tzaddik* of our time, I too have learned to see and hear with this light. And so, thus, I know what is happening in places that are far away from where I may happen to be at any one time—such as your wretched *shtetl* of W.

Shimon had finally calmed his nerves enough to speak in response: So you will help us then? You will come back with me to W., and accept our atonement, and intercede before the Throne of Glory to nullify the terrible decrees that have been issued against us?

Reb Aharon leaned forward and put his hands on Shimon's shoulders. In good time, my friend. Tomorrow at dawn we will leave for W.—*nu*, it is only a day's ride from here, right? Less perhaps? But now we must rejoice. You did not drink your mead. No bother, I will get you some more. You need to drink and to be merry.

Aharon grabbed the empty mug from the table, walked back into the kitchen, and returned a moment later with a full cup of mead.

Drink up! he urged. *L'Chaim!*

I am sorry, Reb Aharon, I am too tired. I need to rest. Today has been a great strain for me.

Nonsense, Aharon replied. What great strain can there be? All around you is the glory of the Creation of the Holy One, Blessed be He. You breathe His fine air, and hear His birds sing. He created everything here, so everything here partakes of His essence. To spurn that mead is to spurn a tiny speck of *HaShem* Himself—something that is both sinful and ungrateful.

Shimon struggled to follow this strange logic—a part of the Lord of the Universe was floating in his mead, waiting to be drunk? To his ears, that was as absurd as the silly ceremony in the Gentile churches where they drink wine and pretend it is the Holy One's blood—as if He had a body somehow.

But still, he remembered that he must show honor and deference to this man, peculiar as he might be. So Shimon answered softly: Reb Aharon, I am no scholar and I have no knowledge of profound mysteries. Your words are far beyond the little Torah I have managed to learn. I only know the few things that my body has taught to my feeble mind, like when my bones need to sleep—and that is what I feel now, that exhaustion in my bones.

Reb Aharon now jumped up and pointed his forefinger almost into Shimon's eye, his face flushed with red fury. You are right, Reb Shimon, you are an ignoramus. So listen well to the words of wisdom I give you: if you do not drink, and sing, and dance, you will sin against and dishonor not just me, but the Holy One Himself. If you want to show me that the Jews of W. are ready to repent of their wicked ways, then you must show me that you too can rejoice in His Glorious Creation.

Shimon now felt a sudden chill of terror: What if he were to offend and drive away Reb Aharon? Then he could be responsible for the death of his Miriam from her sickness, and who could say how many other Jewish children. So he steeled himself, raised his mug, quickly recited the blessing, and drained it to the dregs. After the many grueling fast days he had recently undergone, the alcohol went quickly to his head, and the room spun about in his mind.

Reb Aharon pinched his cheek and smiled. That is more like it! Now dance with me.

Aharon pulled Shimon up from his chair and began to sing a fast, catchy tune with babyish nonsense words—di-di's and ya-ya's and oy-oy's—as if, Shimon thought, he was some deranged toddler. Shimon forced himself to smile and did whatever Aharon wanted him to; he even tried singing the silly baby sounds too.

The peasants fell silent and watched the two dancing Jews, their eyes full of amazement. But after a moment, they began clapping and beating their feet to Aharon's tune, and many of them got up to dance. The whole inn resounded with the exuberant song.

Reb Aharon asked Shimon: Do you feel it now, the glory of His Creation and the wondrous joy that lurks everywhere in this world that He made? Do you feel His presence, His holy sparks, in your feet and in the song?

Shimon was too frightened to do anything other than pretend that his heavy, anxious heart was actually overflowing with happiness. So he smiled widely and swore he had never felt such ecstasy—and offered a secret prayer that his words would find enough favor with Reb Aharon to save his daughter.

VII. Atonement

THE NEXT DAY Reb Shimon and Reb Aharon returned to the *shtetl* of W. Reb Aharon sipped brandy throughout the trip, and often burst into song. From time to time, he ordered the coachman to stop the wagon in the middle of the road so he could climb down and dance by a field for several minutes. He praised the beauty of everything around them—the fields, the trees, the birds, the peasant girls hauling water, the wooden buckets they carried, even the wonder of water itself—everything so lovely and perfect, so full of the divine presence suffusing nature everywhere he turned his eyes.

Shimon's thoughts, however, were fixed on the image of his daughter Miriam soaked in sweat and vomiting uncontrollably. And then he recalled a procession to the graveyard carrying three miniature coffins, each just barely big enough to hold the corpse of a baby struck down by the terrible disease that had ravaged W. These caskets were so small and light that one man from the burial society was able to carry them all by himself, stacked on top of each other like parcels from the butcher. Some parents wailed and screamed as they trailed the pile of little coffins, while others stumbled along with dazed eyes and distracted steps. Tears slowly slid down Shimon's face at these harsh memories.

But then Aharon shot him an angry glance. Shimon quickly forced himself to smile again and then started singing a song, so he could sound joyful without having to speak any words. He had no idea what he was singing until the wagon driver joined in, and at that moment he realized it was a Polish song he had heard drunken peasants sing in his tavern, about the rollicking adventures of a pretty maiden who was loose with her morals—she was doing something shameful with a priest, but Shimon's Polish was not good enough to make out all the lyrics. He blushed deeply but dared not stop his song.

Reb Aharon laughed and smacked him on the back in a jovial way. Shimon wondered if the *tzaddik* knew Polish. He hoped Aharon did not.

In the late afternoon they arrived at Shimon's inn in W. Reb Aharon instructed Shimon to summon the leading Jewish house-holders in the town to gather in the synagogue that evening. In the meantime, he asked Leah to prepare food for him to eat and to pour him more brandy to drink.

Shimon ran about the town frantically rounding up the lead-ing householders and the rabbi. They were overjoyed that he had found the *tzaddik* so soon—a clear sign, they all said, that the Heavenly Court wished to ease their sufferings and lift the harsh decrees against them. At the rabbi's instruction each man rent his garment and they chanted Psalms together in the synagogue while waiting for the holy saint to arrive and address them.

When Reb Aharon entered the synagogue, the rabbi kneeled down upon the ground and kissed his feet. The rabbi then spoke to him in a voice quivering with emotion: Oh great and holy *tzaddik*, please forgive us. We have wronged you, we have shamed you, we have acted wickedly. You are a scholar of the Torah and we treated you worse than a thief or a murderer. We were too foolish and blind to grasp the subtle and penetrating depth of your discourse. We have suffered mightily because of our sins against you. Our children have grown ill and many have died. The *Pan* has levied extortionate fines upon his Jews after he falsely accused us of arson. Please, holy *tzaddik*, forgive us and intercede on our behalf before the Throne of Glory.

After the rabbi had finished speaking, Reb Aharon reached down and lifted him to his feet. He pinched the old man's cheek as if he were a small boy in *cheder* who had done an excellent job reciting the week's lesson. Shimon saw the rage swell in the rabbi's eyes, but it seemed to dissipate before forming into words of rebuke.

Now Reb Aharon spoke: You ask for my forgiveness and you say you have now understood the wisdom of my teachings. These are fine sentiments. But a teacher cannot just take his student's word that the lesson has been mastered. Yes, you have suffered, but have you grown closer to the Holy One, Blessed be He? Tell me, what deeds have you performed that show you merit the lifting of the harsh decrees that hang over this holy community?

The rabbi looked at the ground, sighed, and then answered calmly: We have fasted—we have fasted more days than we have eaten. Through our fasting, we have offered our flesh as an atonement sacrifice. We have prayed, we have sung Psalms. We have confessed our sins wholeheartedly.

Reb Aharon laughed. Do you think I will believe your lies? You call me *tzaddik* and admit that I—I, and not you—have the ability to intercede before the Throne of Glory to plead for mercy. And you think that I, with such deep knowledge of hidden mysteries, would fail to see the rot inside you? The rot that you have concealed from the good Jews in this town and thought you could hide from the eyes of even *HaShem* Himself?

Tell me, Reb Shimon, you are a good and honest Jew, have you been to the rabbi's house?

Shimon did not want to answer, as he was sure his words would somehow be used to shame the rabbi, whom he considered to be an upright and righteous man. But he recalled again how sick his Miriam was; he could not bear the thought that, for want of sufficiently humoring this madman, he had sent her to an early grave.

So he answered: Yes, of course, many times. Our rabbi is like our Father Abraham, a man of generous hospitality. And he always offers counsel and instruction to a Jew with little learning, like myself.

Reb Aharon pressed on: And tell me, Reb Shimon, did the rabbi ever employ a Gentile servant girl in his house?

Shimon furrowed his brow and tried to recall. But then he remembered: Yes, Maryska, Stefan's youngest daughter—Stefan looks after the *Pan*'s horses.

The rabbi, turning pale and shaking, now spoke out angrily: What is the meaning of this, you so-called *tzaddik*? Are you trying to insinuate some slander? Start some vile gossip?

But Reb Aharon kept his gaze firmly fixed on Shimon: While he was fasting and confessing his sins, did the rabbi happen to tell you how many times he has lain with Maryska? No? Well, I can assure you it was as numerous as the stars shining in the sky. This rabbi here tasted such sweet pleasure with her—for him, her soft flesh was a land overflowing with milk and honey. But then the rabbi's seed, alas, found too fertile soil and the lovely maidservant Maryska had to depart for distant relatives where she could birth the rabbi's wretched little *mamzer* in peace.

Reb Shimon, tell me, when this rabbi led you in penitential prayers, as your children cried out in pain and anguish, did he seek forgiveness for these particular sins?

The rabbi reached over and grabbed Reb Aharon's sleeve. Enough! he shouted.

Reb Aharon, however, still refused to look at the rabbi. He instead turned his eyes to the assembly of Jewish householders and addressed them: Gentlemen, fine Jews, can't you see that this filthy lecher is the cause of your sufferings? Every time he sinned—and there were so many, many times—his sin gave birth to a new demon. And not just any demon: because their father was a scholar of vast learning who had committed entire tractates of the Talmud to memory, these demons were unusually strong and powerful. His litter of demon offspring eventually ran amok in your town, first attacking your livestock and then your children. And it was no doubt these demons who whispered such evil counsel into the ears of the *Pan*.

These were the demons who blocked your prayers. All the pleas for mercy that passed your lips in this synagogue were caught in the air and torn apart by this army of demons before they could ascend to the Throne of Glory.

If you truly wish for the Heavenly Court to heed your cries for help and lift its harsh decrees, then you must act. Expel this sinner from your midst. And not only expel him, but show the Holy One and His righteous angels that you realize he deserves none of the honor you have lavished upon him in your ignorance and folly.

In response to these grave accusations, the Jewish householders looked at the ground and breathed heavily. Shimon did not know what to do, and he felt the silence to be a terrible weight crushing his chest.

Then he heard a shout. Reb Aharon, grinning madly, had thrown the old rabbi down onto the floor and was kicking his belly. Yes, look at me, he said to the householders, I am redeeming you from the captivity of this man's sins, I am doing what you should have done long ago. Join me. Kick him, too. Rejoice in seeing how wickedness should be rewarded.

The rabbi, gasping for breath, begged for help.

Shimon pitied the rabbi, and was revolted by the way he was being shamed. But he was also scared of angering Reb Aharon.

As Shimon wavered, he saw Reb Kalman, the butcher, step forward. Kalman was a bear of a man—tall, broad-shouldered, and just slightly plump. Shimon watched Kalman move his eyes between Aharon and the old rabbi. And then Kalman lifted his foot, and smashed his heel down hard on the rabbi's ribs. The old man screamed out in pain.

Now all the Jewish householders joined in, kicking and spitting upon the rabbi. One man even urinated upon him. And Shimon joined in too. He did not want to, at least at first. But he feared that if he were the only householder not to shame the rabbi, then Reb Aharon would let his daughter's suffering rage on without reprieve.

However, once he had started kicking the rabbi, with everyone cheering him on and smiling at him, his heart became light and beat excitedly, and he had a giddy, dizzy feeling as if he were dancing and tipsy. Before he knew it he had lost track of how many blows he had landed upon the bleeding old man moaning and writhing on the floor.

Eventually Reb Aharon ordered a halt to the beating. The elderly rabbi was by then unconscious; his eyes were sealed shut beneath hideous purple bruises, his clothes were ripped to shreds, and his body was covered in tracks of dried blood.

Reb Aharon told the Jewish householders to return to their homes and not to venture outside again until the sun rose the next morning.

As if waking from a fevered dream, Shimon was stunned and ashamed at the brutality that he had displayed—as if he were a drunken animal, a filthy boar running wild through the synagogue and goring the innocent with his sharp tusks. The rabbi had been kind to him through the years. He had eaten many meals at the old man's table, and had sought the rabbi's advice when he and Leah fought terribly in the first year of their marriage. So it turned out that the man had his secret weakness and folly—who doesn't?

That is why the Gates of Repentance must be open to everyone, always, as this is the greatest and truest sign of the Holy One's love and mercy. The old rabbi should have been treated as a sinner in need of penitence, not as a rabid dog to be put down.

And Shimon had cruelly betrayed him, first out of craven fear, and then out of a lust for violence, a terrible sin that he did not realize was even inside him. Feeling a stabbing pain in his heart at the memory of the image of the bloodied little old man lying unconscious on the synagogue floor, eyes buried underneath bulging purple bruises, Shimon swore to himself that he would beg the rabbi's forgiveness the next morning and undertake whatever atonement he was ordered to suffer.

But the next morning, the old rabbi was nowhere to be found. His house had been burned to the ground, his possessions were gone, and no one knew his whereabouts. And Shimon did not dare ask Reb Aharon.

VIII. Blessings

IN THE DAYS that followed, the children of the Jews of the *shtetl* of W. made a miraculous recovery; within three days of Reb Aharon's arrival in town, each child was not only cured, but strong, laughing, and bursting with playful energy. The remaining live-stock, too, were cured and the cows and the goats were now bursting with rich, sweet milk. The extraordinary cheese and butter made from this milk soon became famous throughout Poland, causing the Jews of W. to prosper.

And the *Pan* lifted his harsh decree. The day after Reb Aharon's arrival in W., the *Pan* had received a cache of letters from an anonymous sender. These letters were the correspondence be-tween two Christian priests who were notorious for their heretical views and lax morals, leading them both to be severely disciplined by the local bishop. In revenge, they had made a pact with a de-mon to burn down the church, the convent, and the *Pan*'s private chapel, as the bishop was the *Pan*'s younger brother.

Confronted with such clear evidence as to who the true guilty parties were, the *Pan* once again summoned the leading Jewish householders (including Shimon) to his estate, but now admitted that the Jews were not the wicked men whom he had thought they were. He apologized for having been too quick to anger, and, to make amends, pledged many ducats to repair the ageing synagogue and *bet midrash*.

Even Ivan's dog rubbed his head lovingly against the legs of the Jewish visitors, and submissively licked Shimon's palm.

Reb Shimon could hardly believe the blessings that had been showered upon W.'s Jews since Reb Aharon's return. He had heard tales of how, in the distant past, the Holy One, Blessed be He, had miraculously saved His People Israel from terrible dangers but he had never quite fully believed in them—it had seemed too childish and silly to believe that wicked persecutors could suddenly change their minds about everything in the world and become righteous defenders of the innocent. But now that he had seen such marvels with his own eyes, he felt ashamed of his earlier doubts.

But still, he did not understand why the old rabbi had to be beaten and humiliated. Yes, he had been mistaken in his initial opinion of Reb Aharon, but he had repented of his sins and had nearly killed himself with fasting. Couldn't Reb Aharon have offered just a small pinch of compassion?

No one would speak of the old rabbi. Shimon had tried asking the other Jewish householders about what had happened to the rabbi, but as soon as the words passed his lips, the other Jews would stare at the ground, suddenly recall the need to attend to urgent matters of business, and hurriedly shuffle away.

Seeking the wisdom to understand what was happening in W., Reb Shimon attended the sermons that Reb Aharon now gave in the *bet midrash*. He was not alone: it seemed that every Jew in the town wished to know the teachings of the man who had brought them so many blessings.

Reb Aharon was an unusual teacher. He did not give carefully prepared sermons, with detailed written notes and meticulously cited proof texts, in the manner of the old rabbi and the other scholars who had lectured in the town in years past. Rather, he would sit at the end of a bench, swaying over the *Zohar*, until a large enough crowd had gathered. Then he would look up, see the sun was setting, and carefully close the volume he had been studying.

The discourse would always begin the same way: Aharon would ask three of the assembled men to each quote the first lines of Bible or Talmud that came into their minds. Three utterly disjointed phrases would issue forth. Reb Aharon would then launch into an extemporaneous commentary linking the passages together and revealing their hidden, unified core of truth.

Unlike the householders, Aharon spoke freely and openly of the former rabbi. He taught that the rabbi had foolishly assumed that learning and study were the same as holiness and piety. He had held himself apart from—no, worse, he thought himself better than, even superior to—the beauty of the Creation of the Holy One, Blessed be He, spurning food, drink, song, dance, and other pleasures in favor of constant fasts and solitude as he mulled commentaries upon the most minute, abstruse intricacies of the Talmud. Thus alienated from the divine presence all around him in the Holy One's Creation, the starved, light-headed rabbi became easy prey for the sensual visions that Lilith, Queen of the Demons, dangled before his eyes. The harder the rabbi would strain in the dim candlelight to make out the tiny printed Aramaic words, the more images he would be shown by Lilith of her alluring daughters dancing wantonly in the shadows. It was sadly only a matter of time before these demonic lusts overwhelmed him and he fell into sin with his Gentile maidservant.

Reb Aharon would then continue with his advice on how to avoid such a terrible fate: The divine presence, he would teach, is everywhere around us. The Holy One, Blessed be He, in His Infinite and Abounding Kindness and Wisdom, chose to create the world from His own essence and thus this world is part of Him— as we are all part of Him, as we too are but His creations in His perfect image. To avoid the lures and snares of the forces of evil, a Jew must grow closer to the Holy One, which means growing closer to His Creation, for His Creation is but an extension of Himself.

At this point Reb Aharon's eyes would light up with passion and he would rise to his feet. His hands would wave wildly about and sometimes slam down hard upon the table, as he would speak his words of wisdom for upright living: You must abandon the illusion, spread by the forces of evil and sin, that you are beings who exist separate and apart from the Creation all around you. You must destroy yourself; you must negate yourself so that you dissolve your soul into the divine presence that inheres in everything surrounding you. Lose yourself in food and drink, for these are joys and delights He created for you. Lose yourself in song and dance, faster and faster, so that your mind is no longer plotting and weaving and worrying, but instead you have no sense of being anyone at all, just a tiny piece of the great divine, holy song that is the world He created.

Reb Shimon found these doctrines to be strange. All his life holy men, especially those who had plumbed the depths of the secret wisdom of the *Kabbalah*, had been ascetics who fasted and mortified themselves so much that their skeletal frames could barely stand upright. These saints had big round eyes staring into faraway, vacant distances. And when they spoke with their thin, rasping voices, it was as if they were addressing celestial spheres and heavenly hosts, and not the person next to them. They could not have danced in ecstasy even if they had tried, and a tall glass of vodka would have burned their fragile insides to a crisp.

Shimon recalled one man in particular, an itinerant *baal shem* whom the old rabbi had invited to W. many years back when there was a fear that a girl in town had been possessed by the wandering spirit of a sinner, a *dybbuk*. It was winter then, and the snows were deep. Shimon had offered this man a fine, warm room in his inn, with thick blankets, but the man had refused his hospitality. Instead he slept barefoot in the snow, to the point where his feet turned dark blue and several of his frostbitten toes had to be cut off.

Shimon had understood that these afflictions upon the body were necessary to achieve a holiness in spirit, to free the soul from the appetites and needs of the lowly physical body so that it could ascend to higher realms. How exactly this was done he could not say; he lacked the learning to know such things. But he had trusted in the old rabbi's assurance that this self-torturing ascetic had been a great saint.

And now Reb Aharon preached that saintliness was singing, drunkenness, and gluttony, by which measure every smelly, cursing peasant on the *Pan*'s estates was a holy man. Yet the rabbi's ways had brought only disaster, and this new preacher had brought so many wonderful blessings. So who was Reb Shimon to say he was wrong?

After one of his discourses, Reb Aharon announced that he had lingered too long in W. He must return, he said, to his master and teacher, the holy Maggid of M. Reb Aharon insisted he himself had no wisdom to offer but what crumbs he had lovingly gathered from the remains of the Maggid's magnificent, plentiful feasts. However, he continued, he had been sent forth by the holy Maggid to raise funds and recruit new disciples to learn the true Torah at the Maggid's court. He would be embarrassed to return empty-handed from W., having spent so much time in the town.

The householders immediately opened their purses and gave generously to Reb Aharon. They also offered up their sons to travel with him to the court of the holy Maggid of M., to learn this marvelous and penetrating new wisdom from the source.

Reb Aharon now began his preparations for this group of new, young disciples to leave for their pilgrimage to the Maggid. He insisted that, as a first step, the young men who were to travel with him must take rooms at Shimon's inn, and leave their fathers' houses.

And so it came to pass that Shimon's inn was filled to the brim with Aharon and his band of disciples. When Shimon asked how long they intended to stay, Reb Aharon explained that it would take time for his new students to be ready to hear the truths of the Torah directly from the lips of the holy Maggid of M. It is as if, he said, a man had spent his entire life in a pitch dark cave. To take him out immediately into the bright noonday sun will over-whelm him, and he will not see—he will shut his eyes tightly in pain from so much unaccustomed light. He needs to learn to see first by a dim candlelight in the darkness before he can be taken into the bright sunshine. Reb Aharon would need several weeks to help these young men see by the dim candlelight of his simple teachings before they could face the Maggid's blinding light.

IX. Sin

SHIMON HAD MARRIED his Leah many years ago. He considered himself fortunate in this match: she was prudent, hard-working, and, of no small importance to an innkeeper, a talented cook. He had heard traveling merchants tell stories of men and women who desired each other feverishly, like cats in heat, usually leading to a bad end when the husband of the one or the wife of the other got wind of what was happening. He had never felt such feral passion for Leah, and he was sure she had never felt that way about him either. But she was as solid as the earth beneath his feet: a woman he could trust, a steady and wise partner in his endeavors.

And because of this deep trust, he at first thought nothing of her strange absences at night. After all, some nights she would be up late cleaning the dishes or arranging the tables in the tavern. Or making sure the guests' horses were properly fed and watered in the stables. Or mending clothes. Or maybe just going for a walk if the air was mild because doesn't everyone, his wife included, deserve a break every so often to breathe in the fresh air and stretch her legs?

Although these thoughts calmed his mind for a time, he eventually grew concerned when her absences stretched on night after night. He would see her during the day, cooking, caring for

Miriam, cleaning up, chattering with the guests, arguing with who-
ever was selling something, just as she always did. But once night
came, she vanished.

One day, when they were both hard at work in the kitchen, he
asked to speak to her. She looked suddenly nervous, and Shimon
noticed there were purple bruises on the side of her neck, like a
demon's thumbprints. But as he leaned forward, to take her hand
and lead her to a corner where they could speak privately, Leah
said she had just remembered that they were almost out of chicken
feet for the soup, and also flour for the honey cakes, and she
needed to run and buy these and much else besides before the
shops closed in town. Before he knew it, Leah had run off and was
out of his sight.

Shimon did not see Leah again that day, or later that night.

The next morning, he saw her again in the kitchen. Once
more, he asked gently if he could have a word with her, but she
said she did not have the time, that there was too much to do—
hungry guests needed their breakfast. And afterwards, every time
he saw her somewhere, and began to approach, she slipped away as
if she existed only in fleeting glances from the corner of his eye.

Confused and frustrated, Shimon decided he would secretly
follow Leah, to see where she went and what she was doing during
these mysterious nighttime disappearances. As they were cleaning
the tables that evening after Reb Aharon and his many disciples
had eaten their full at dinner, Shimon kept a close eye on Leah.
After a while she left the tavern and went outside; he quietly
followed.

The moon was just bright enough for him to make out her
silhouette in the distance. She walked away from the inn, past the
stables, and into the old barn at the far end of the property.
Shimon used this building to store supplies, and sometimes, when
wealthy lords or merchants passed through with large retinues, he
would arrange for the servants to sleep on the haystacks there.

After she had entered the barn, Shimon went around to the back, where he knew there were holes in the wall (lucky for him, he thought, that he had been so absentminded about getting them repaired). Peering through one such hole, he saw that Leah had lit a candle and placed it on a small wooden table. She was standing in the middle of the barn, very still.

Shimon now thought he understood the mystery: she was waiting for a lover. This was exactly like those stories the traveling merchants would tell him of wives swept away by their lusts, who took secret lovers and humiliated their husbands through their lies and treacheries. He grew angry—how could she betray him so? And why—hadn't he been a good husband to her? Hadn't he saved their Miriam's life by bringing Reb Aharon back to W. and getting the plague or curse or whatever it was lifted? Filthy whore, his thoughts continued, while he had struggled to save their daughter's life, she had rolled in the haystacks with her lover.

He pictured this lover in his mind: not a Jew, not a scholar, but a big, oafish lout of a peasant, some blond-haired, big-shouldered serf with vodka on his breath—the kind of man whom it was easy to confuse with a beast, like an ox or maybe a bear. Yes, her lover was not even a *goyische* peasant; he was a bear. The filthy whore gave her body willingly to a sweaty bear, so debased was she in her lusts.

But then his eyes noticed something that stopped his rampaging imagination in its tracks: Leah did not look happy. While he had not thought much about the matter, he had always assumed that a woman consumed by bodily passions would be excited, eager, for a tryst with her lover. But Leah looked as if she had just been told that her parents had died.

Shimon looked again. She was trembling—she was not only sad, she was scared. There were tears falling down her cheeks. What kind of secret meeting was this? And if she were so sad and frightened, why run away from her husband who could help her?

Then another person, a man, entered the barn. From his dress, he was clearly a Jew but the man was standing too far from the light for Shimon to see his face. Leah looked at this man, nodded, and without saying a word, removed her wig and then her clothes.

The man also undressed. Leah averted her eyes from his naked body; she was red with shame.

The man now approached close enough to Leah that his face could be seen in the light cast by the candle. To Shimon's shock, it was Reb Aharon. He grabbed her neck from behind, pressing his thumb hard into the place where Shimon had earlier seen the purple bruises. He bent her over and did what men do in their lusts, but in a way that resembled a male dog mounting its mate in a garbage-strewn alley. Still, Aharon smiled broadly and seemed pleased with himself.

Leah continued to look distressed, but she did not resist or protest. She closed her eyes and mumbled something—perhaps a prayer?

It was over quickly. After he had done what he came to do, Reb Aharon dressed again at a leisurely pace, whistling and singing nonsense words to one of his fast-paced melodies. Leah meanwhile had collapsed onto the ground and was sobbing.

Aharon sternly rebuked her: Such sadness is a great sin. You are immersed in the beauty of Creation, amidst the many miraculous divine sparks of the Holy One, Blessed be He. Everything that exists is from Him, is part of Him, and thus is good. To denounce and accuse the things of this world with your tears is therefore to blaspheme and insult the Holy One. You will have to atone later for your behavior tonight. But for now, I must return to my disciples.

And with that he left, seemingly indifferent to whether Leah replied or not.

Shimon now ran inside the barn. When Leah saw him, still naked, weeping and shivering, she covered her head with her hands and squeezed herself into a tight ball. He knew she was deeply ashamed, but his rage was so overwhelming that he did not care.

How could you lie with another man? he asked. How could you betray me this way? For how long have you been degrading yourself?

Leah answered haltingly between sobs: How could I say no? He came to me, and he demanded it. I wanted to say no, but then I remembered how sick our Miriam had been, how she had almost died. And that sickness had been the result of his wrath, the offense to his honor and dignity. So many children had died to appease his anger. If I had said no, would he have cursed and afflicted Miriam again? Might she die this time? What could I do?

Shimon's anger now melted away, and he felt guilty for his earlier cruelty. He gathered up Leah's clothes from the floor and silently helped her to dress again. He held her hand as they walked back to the inn, although they avoided each other's eyes.

X. The Parable and its Lesson

SHIMON COULD NOT sleep that night. He thought: How could a holy *tzaddik* abuse and shame a Jewish wife this way? Maybe his power came not from the Holy One, Blessed be He, but from hideous demons that he knew how to bend to his will. The Poles in his tavern would swap stories of witches who copulated with demons and spread disease and pestilence, especially towards children, to force their will upon others. Maybe Reb Aharon was such a witch, except— may it never happen again—a witch who was also a rabbi.

When he saw Reb Aharon on his way to prayers the next morning, Shimon could not control himself. The sight of him, well rested, smiling and humming, as if nothing were amiss in the universe, was too much of an insult to bear.

Shimon lunged at him and pinned him against the wall.

I saw you last night, he said, in the barn, I saw what you did to my Leah. How can you call yourself a *tzaddik*? How can you sit in judgment upon our rabbi, when you are … you are … Leave, I want you to leave. And stop shaming my wife, she is a good woman, a righteous woman.

Reb Aharon stayed quite calm, except that his eyes seemed to smolder with something—not rage exactly, but some heightened awareness and sensation. He responded serenely: There are many demonic forces in this world, and they cloud and deceive our gullible minds. You think you have seen, and you think you have understood. But you have not. Still, I will not grow angry with you. In these matters, in true, hidden matters, you are like a child, because there has been no master here to teach you the wisdom necessary for you to grow into a man.

You are fortunate that I am a kind man and that I am taking pity upon you. I want you to understand. So I will teach you. Before I depart with my disciples to study at the court of the holy Maggid of M.—may his merit protect us—I will teach you, and you will learn.

And with that, Reb Aharon pried himself loose from Shimon's grip and left the inn to go attend to his morning prayers.

Reb Aharon did not return until after dark, but by then Shimon was in no state to confront him again. Immediately after the midday meal he had begun vomiting uncontrollably, eventually falling to the ground in a pool of his own upturned fluids. Too weak to stand back up on his own, he called out for help as best he could until the stable hand, a ruddy and strong Ukrainian, came by and carried him to a mattress on the kitchen floor.

After the nausea had passed, Shimon was overwhelmed by a burning fever, a tight pain in his chest that made breathing difficult, and a pounding in his head, like a hammer smashing his skull. His fingers and toes swelled monstrously, and hives cropped up all over his legs and back.

When Leah saw him, she fell to her knees. Please forgive me, she said, this is my doing, a result of my wicked sins and lies. First Miriam, now you. He is angry about what you saw, and he is punishing you. We must beg his forgiveness. I will beg his forgiveness. I will offer to do anything for him if he will release you from this suffering, as he released our Miriam. I am wretched, I am disgusting, I bring misery and curses wherever I go.

Shimon could hear and understand her words, but he could no longer speak in response. He wanted to tell her not to dishonor herself any further, even if it meant his soul would depart from his body—this world is a fleeting illusion anyway, and they could live properly as husband and wife together someday in the World to Come. But the words evaporated in his throat and never made it past his lips.

Leah had him moved to his actual bed. There she and Miriam cared for him: they brought him chicken broth and soft bread and sweet brandy, they washed him, they changed his clothes and his sheets. They spoke soothing, loving words to him—kind words of hope and concern and affection.

Days passed as Shimon drifted in and out of consciousness, too weak to move from his bed. He once thought he saw the angel of death at the foot of his bed, with his long knife and hundred eyes. Shimon closed his eyes and prayed fervently to be taken from this world into the next, so that his sufferings could finally be at an end. But when he opened his eyes again, the angel of death had disappeared. He had seemingly been cursed to be suspended, mute and delirious, between the two worlds—this lowly world and the World to Come.

One day Reb Aharon came to visit. The holy *tzaddik* spoke to him:

Reb Shimon, I know that you are unwell and that you have lost the power of speech. While you must find your suffering to be unbearable, you should know that it is the will of the Holy One, Blessed be He, that, for now, you are to be so bitterly afflicted. But Our Lord is a Lord of Mercy as well as a Lord of Vengeance, and His mercy will return to you and it will heal you. Soon enough, you shall walk again, and talk again, and eat and drink again, and you will struggle to remember what this illness felt like—it will be like a fleeting dream that dissolves into the air when you try to touch it.

But everything the Lord does has a purpose and a reason, and your sickness too has a purpose and a reason. You have lived your life sunk in lies that you were told to believe not only as if they were truths, but as if they were truths from the holy Torah itself. Your soul even fell into such mad confusion that you assaulted and slandered me—I, who should be your teacher, I, to whom you should show nothing but honor and deference. You should wash my boots in gratitude for the wisdom and learning that I wish to impart to you.

But I forgive you. You do not know what you do not know.

Now, at last, I shall teach you.

Where shall we begin? It is important to meet each pupil where he is, with just the right amount of learning that he can handle at that particular moment in time—try to pour too much knowledge down your throat too fast and you will gag and wheeze and spit it all back up. So where are you as a pupil, right here, right now?

You are firmly convinced that your former rabbi and I are alike in sin. This is the root of your error, and so this is where the lesson should start.

Your rabbi believed the world around him was polluted and evil. Thus, according to his thinking, fasting was a righteous deed because the food of this world is gross and material and weighted him down, and without its leaden heaviness his soul would be free to float up and ascend to the higher realms where the Divine Presence dwells. He isolated himself from the world—no drinking, no dancing, no rejoicing, just constant fasting and long hours of study by the light of a dim candle in a moldy, stale room.

These notions of his—which he taught to you as if they were the most obvious truths—were grave, foolish errors. Everything around us was created by the Holy One, Blessed be He, and thus everything partakes of Him—in everything there is a spark of His holiness. Those sparks are in our food and drink, they are in our songs, they are in the birds and the beasts and the trees, and the warm sun and the cold rains. He is everywhere around us, and inside each of us too—for we, like the bees and the wheat and the raindrops, are His creations and we too, each of us, therefore carry a spark of His holy perfection.

But your rabbi spurned this glorious Creation filled with the Divine Presence, spurned food and drink and song, and so while he thought he was seeking holiness, he actually fled far, far away from it. Do you recall how, when you fast for a whole day, your head becomes dizzy and light and full of dull pains, and your thoughts simply will not form clearly? That is because the fasting made you grow distant from the divine sparks all around you—the more you flee from them, the more your thoughts are clouded and confused.

To what can this be compared? It is like a king who builds a great capital city, with a vast palace in the center. The king seeks ministers to help him rule justly and wisely. One of these ministers swears he will serve the king better than any of the others, anticipating and satisfying his sovereign's every desire, no matter how trivial or small. But this particular minister also believes that the only way to serve his lord so fully and deeply is to flee the king's capital city, run away, alone, to a distant desert, and boast to the scorpions about how much he loves his king and how hard at work he is serving him. Wouldn't you agree that this minister is a contemptible fool? Such was your rabbi.

And do you know who these scorpions in the desert were to whom your rabbi addressed his exalted, fine words? The demon queen Lilith and her daughters. And they whispered back into his ears about the comeliness of his Gentile maidservant. They extolled her beauty and said she was the beloved from the Song of Songs. With his vision blurred by the sand blown in his eyes by the hot desert winds, your rabbi fell into the demons' trap and sinned.

I can see from your eyes that you agree with me, at least this far into the lesson. Good, that is very good, you are learning. As your teacher, I am pleased.

But now you wish to ask me a question. Because the Holy One, Blessed be He, has, for the time being, removed the blessing of speech from your lips, I must speak on behalf of the pupil as well as the teacher.

If you could speak, you would ask: But didn't Lilith whisper evil words into your ears, too, Reb Aharon? Isn't that why you embraced my wife Leah? How can you speak ill of our former rabbi when you are no different yourself?

Reb Shimon, my fine and eager pupil, I am glad you have asked the questions you did, because it will take us to the heart of the matter.

In the beginning there was nothing but the Holy One Himself, Whose presence filled the entire universe—He was so infinite and vast that there was not room for anything else to exist. And then, in His Mercy and Goodness, He contracted Himself to make room for Creation. But in order for that Creation to come to life and to flourish, He had to fill it with sparks of His Holiness. Those sparks are all around us.

It is not possible for the Holy One, Blessed be He, to sin. After all, the Torah comes from Him and contains His essence. Whatever emanates from the Master of the Universe is, without doubt, righteous and good.

Unlike your former rabbi, I have not withdrawn myself from the holy Creation around me. I have opened my soul to the Divine Presence to the point that I no longer feel there is any individual self in me distinct from the rest of the Creation. As all things, including my soul, draw their sustenance from His divine sparks, then we are all simply pieces of Him, one enormous unity. I have dissolved myself into His perfection and wholeness.

Thus, whatever desires I feel are holy, because they can only come from the Divine Presence. As there is no I who is separate from Him, then my yearnings are solely what the Holy One wills, for whatever mysterious reasons of His own. Hence, when I saw your wife Leah and my blood boiled with desire, I knew that this was what the Holy One, Blessed be He, had decreed and desired, because otherwise these impulses and lusts could not have arisen within me. In order to serve Him and to do His will, I humbly obeyed the cravings that He had made flow through my body. It is a great sin to scorn the commands of the Master of the Universe.

Your Leah, alas, has had trouble understanding these matters. She submits to His will, but she does so with sadness, and not with the joy and happiness that should accompany performing the Holy One's commandments and thereby growing closer to Him. She is confused, poor woman, just like you—for far too many years have false teachings been spoken to her as if they were the truth.

It is as if she were a princess—for all the children of Israel are royalty—who had been exiled from her father's palace as an infant and raised by birds in the forest. These birds had kind hearts, but they only knew how to feed their own chicks with worms, and so that is what they fed the little princess too. Thus, year after year, she grew up eating nothing but worms.

But one day a nobleman goes hunting in that very same forest. He meets and recognizes the princess because, dirty and disheveled though she may be, her inner royalty shines through her beaming eyes. The nobleman rescues her, and takes her back to his luxurious pavilion. He orders his servants to serve the princess only the finest delicacies. But because she has only eaten worms before, she is revolted by the fine food and thinks she is being mistreated, maybe even poisoned. She needs to learn how to live like a true princess, and not a beast in the forest.

Your eyes still appear skeptical. I understand these matters can be difficult to grasp. Let me tell you another tale, which will help to illuminate the truth, this tale being from my own life. When I was young, I studied the Law day and night. I painstakingly parsed the tractates of the Talmud and their many commentaries, and I crafted the most exacting, hairsplitting arguments. I was quite impressed with myself, even though I did not know or understand my Creator and His will. I had simply mastered cunning verbal tricks to awe and intimidate the less learned and to make them fawn over me as if I were an idol to be worshipped.

Then I heard rumors of a great scholar, the holy Maggid of M., who taught a wisdom that could not be found in any of the commentaries. My overweening vanity made me want to learn this wisdom too. I journeyed to M. and arrived at the Maggid's court on a Friday afternoon, a couple of hours before the sun set and *Shabbat* began. At dinner that night, the Maggid was dressed in blindingly bright white robes and he had a long flowing white beard and radiant blue eyes—he shined brilliantly like the Divine Presence.

He called out to each new guest by name, including me, even though none of us had ever met him before. Then he asked each of us to quote the first verses of Bible or Talmud that came to our minds. As you can imagine, we quoted verses that had seemingly no connections with each other—a Psalm here, a passage from Leviticus there, I think someone may even have babbled a bit of the Book of Esther. Yet the Maggid strung these verses together in the most wondrous and clear interpretations. Subtle connections were revealed beneath the disparate surface meanings, and the lesson was clear: what had appeared to us, in our ignorance, as disjoined verses were, properly understood, part of one unified whole.

After the *Shabbat* ended, I begged the Maggid to let me stay with him and study more of his teachings. In his kindness and pity for me, he agreed. I spent the next several weeks listening closely to the Maggid's words and interpretations. I prayed with his *minyan* in his manner—not the somber and melancholy prayers to which I was accustomed, but vibrant, lively prayers, full of music, dancing, and celebration. He was the teacher who taught me that everything around us is holy and contains a spark of divinity, and that we must negate our individual selves to join with these divine sparks and celebrate the wonder of His Creation.

In my arrogance, I thought that I had imbibed the essence of the holy Maggid's wisdom. But I had not. He had one more lesson to teach me, and it was not easy or simple.

One day I overslept. Who can remember why such things happen—maybe I drank too much brandy the night before, or maybe my sleep had been interrupted by sharp pains in my leg during the night. Whatever it was, I was so late to the morning prayers that everyone else, the Maggid included, was already finished by the time I got there.

The Maggid greeted me when I arrived, and I greeted him. Then suddenly something strange flashed in his eyes. He ordered his other disciples to tie me up with some rope. Trusting my master completely, I did not resist. Once I was bound, he ripped away the shirt from my back, grabbed a whip, and began to beat me. The other disciples stood around in stunned silence. The pain soon became unbearable and I begged him to stop.

But rather than stop, he started to sing a joyous melody. He demanded that the other disciples sing along to the same melody, join their hands and shoulders, and dance happily in a circle around us. And while they sang and they danced, he continued to beat me. I could feel the blood run down my back like quick rushing little rivers, and I heard the drops fall rapidly onto the ground.

I grew weaker and weaker until eventually I collapsed onto the ground. The Maggid now put his whip down and started to kick me with his boots, in my belly, in my ribs. Then he kicked my forehead repeatedly until so much blood gushed down into my eyes that it nearly blinded me. And all this time, the disciples' joyous singing and dancing continued around me.

I was certain that my soul was about to depart from my body, and that the portion of my allotted days had run out. But then suddenly the holy Maggid stopped. He ordered me to be untied and taken to my bed.

Once I had been carefully laid down on the mattress, the Maggid removed a tiny purse from his pocket. And from this purse, he removed one single item, a single green leaf. He touched this leaf to my forehead, and then put it back away. All my wounds were immediately healed and I had never felt stronger or healthier. For that leaf, as I later learned, was from the Garden of Eden and had been gifted to the holy Maggid by the Prophet Elijah on one of my master's many ascents to the higher realms.

And so began my new routine. Each day I was bound and beaten by the Maggid while his disciples sang and danced around me in ecstatic celebration. I would beg and plead for mercy, but he would not relent until I was on the verge of death, at which point I would be healed with the magic leaf. This went on for many days.

Until one day, instead of crying for help, I joined in the Maggid's joyous song. Between the lashes of the whip I sang out ecstatically, and I smiled and I praised my Creator. I had ceased to notice the pain, or to feel anything at all, because I had lost myself completely in the whirl of the song and I had let myself be dissolved into the rapture around me.

The holy Maggid then stopped beating me, and he healed me one last time with the magical leaf. Feeling strong and healthy again, I sang the Song of Songs in the Maggid's special, mystical melody. When I was finished, the Maggid embraced me and kissed my cheek and my forehead. You have finally learned what you had left to learn, he said.

And I understood his lesson: that my body's pain and my preening sense of individual injustice were merely illusions, lies, concealing the hidden unity and holiness of the world around me. The Maggid's desire to beat me and my physical sufferings were all part of one Creation, and as all Creation emanates from the Holy One, Blessed be He, and contains sparks of His Holiness, then this desire to hurt me and those pains that I felt both must have had their wellspring in holiness and be pieces of the divine whole that surrounds us. Nothing can exist without the Holy One, and thus everything that is, is good and righteous and holy. That is the parable and its lesson.

So now you understand that what you witnessed in the barn was not sin, but holiness. There is no reason to be angry, but rather rejoice and praise Him and His wondrous world that He created for us in all its splendor and beauty.

With those words, Reb Aharon, looking quite pleased with himself, exited the room. Reb Shimon, exhausted from the strain of trying to follow the thread of the arguments of the *tzaddik*'s long monologue, fell into a deep sleep.

When he woke, he felt well again, as healthy as if he had never been ill. He jumped up briskly out of bed, dressed, and wandered about the inn until he found Miriam.

Are you feeling better, *tate*? she asked.

Yes, he replied. Where are Reb Aharon and the other guests?

They departed yesterday, for the town for M., to study with the famous Maggid. The young men were very excited for the journey. Reb Aharon told them they were finally ready to learn the Maggid's deep wisdom and profound Torah from the great master's own holy lips.

Shimon nodded absently. And where is your mother? he asked.

She went to the butcher shop. Reb Aharon and his pupils ate all our meat last night.

Shimon quietly thanked her, and walked away. His mind was a jumble. He went outside and strolled around until he got his bearings again, and then he went inside the barn to get a bit of relief from the hot sun.

He sat down in the barn in the precise spot where he had seen Leah fornicate with Aharon. He felt, at that moment, tiny and helpless before the awesome might of his Creator. But there was no joy in his heart, and no song on his lips, just a bitter, hopeless despair that flooded his whole being.

Other Books by Barak Bassman

Elegy of the Minotaur

Repentance: A Tale of Demons in Old Jewish Poland

King Solomon and Ashmedai: A Wisdom Tale

The Twilight of the Magical Siren: A Tale of Late Antiquity

The Leper Princess and The Court Jew

The Last Confession of Joseph della Reina

The Gifts of the Fairy Melusine

Necromancy of the Demon Maiden:
A Gothic Tale of Podolia

The Death of the Wizard Merlin

The Vampire and the The Wandering Jew

www.ingramcontent.com/pod-product-compliance
Lightning Source LLC
Chambersburg PA
CBHW021744190726
48288CB00009B/3153